St

Princesses

Series editor: Lesley Sims
Reading Consultant: Alison Kelly
Roehampton University

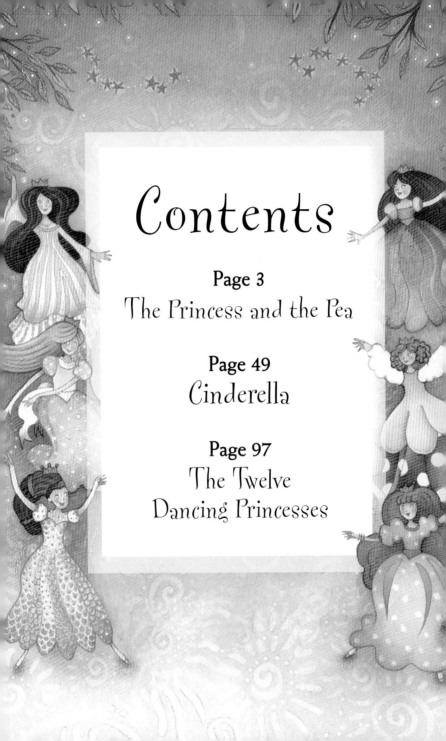

Contents

The Princess and the Pea

Retold by Susanna Davidson

Illustrated by
Mike Gordon

Designed by Russell Punter
and Natacha Goransky

Contents

Chapter 1

The picky prince

Once upon a time there was a prince who wanted to marry a princess. But he didn't want just any old princess. He wanted a *real* one.

This is Princess Cordelia, Your Highness.

Not one of the local princesses would do.

"What's the matter with them, Patrick?" cried his father, the king. "I'm running out of princesses to show you."

Are they too old? Too tall? Too hairy?

"I can't be sure they're real," sighed Prince Patrick. "I'll have to find one for myself."

"You must do whatever you want, darling," said the queen, who spoiled him rotten.

The next day Prince Patrick set out to travel the world, in search of a real princess.

He took with him twelve suitcases, ten pairs of shoes, a spare crown and his cousin, Fred.

"Goodbye, my love," cried the queen, wiping away a tear with her silk handkerchief.

They hadn't gone far when they heard a loud sneeze from under the seat.

"Who's there?" shouted the prince.

A small figure crept out.

It's Peg!

"Aren't you the palace maid?" said Prince Patrick.

Peg nodded.

"Well, what are you doing here?" the prince asked.

"I want to see the world," said Peg. "I've been at the palace all my life – ever since I was left on the doorstep as a baby."

I want an adventure!

She blushed. "And Cook's furious because I burned the pudding," she added.

"Well you can't come with us," said Fred. "This is a boys-only adventure."

You'll get scared and want to go home.

No I won't! I'm as brave as you.

"We're not turning back now," said Prince Patrick. "She'll have to join us."

Peg grinned at Fred.

"OK," Prince Patrick went on. "First stop, the wicked witch's hut."

Fred looked alarmed. "You are joking?"

Prince Patrick shook his head. "The witch will know how to find a real princess. She's my best hope..."

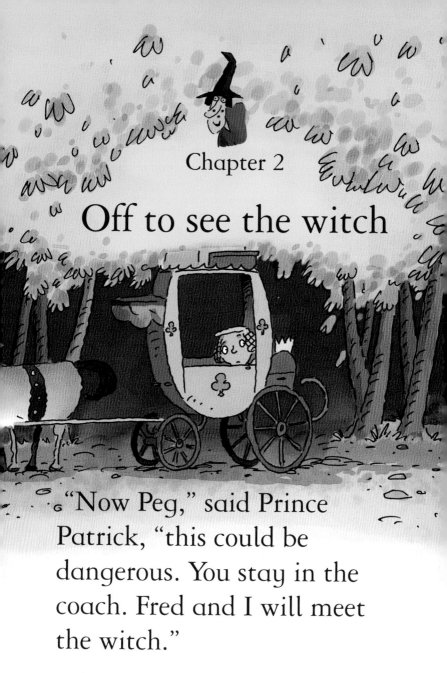

Chapter 2

Off to see the witch

"Now Peg," said Prince Patrick, "this could be dangerous. You stay in the coach. Fred and I will meet the witch."

The prince knocked three
times on the witch's door...
There was no answer.

Why couldn't
I stay in the
coach?

"Looks like no one's in. We'll
have to go," said Fred, who was
already backing away.

13

"She must be in," said the prince, and he bent down to peer through the keyhole.

Argh!

A large green eye was staring at him. Prince Patrick jumped back and landed bottom-first in a patch of mud.

14

A short plump woman opened the door, chuckling to herself. "Did I scare you? I was just checking who you were. You can't be too careful these days."

Look at this mud!

Fred was amazed. "Are you the witch?" he asked. "You're not scary at all."

The witch looked rather upset. "I try my best," she sighed. "I grew three new warts last week."

"Come inside," she added. "I'm just cooking some tasty soup for lunch."

"We're not hungry," said Prince Patrick quickly. "I've come to ask for your help. I want to know how to find a real princess."

"Real princesses are very rare," said the witch, "and it's hard to spot a fake one. But there is a test you can do."

Let me see...

"A real princess must have... boiled brains, rotten beans and cat spit."

"What?" cried the prince.

"Oh sorry, that's a recipe for soup. This is it..."

17

The real princess test

A real princess must possess ...

1. Politeness
   to one and all

2. Kindness
   to rich and poor

3. Very sensitive
   skin

"Sensitive skin?" Prince
Patrick asked, looking confused.

"A real princess," explained
the witch, "has such tender skin
that she could feel a pea under
twenty mattresses."

"Thank you," said the prince. "You've been very helpful." He turned to the door.

"Oh do stay for lunch," pleaded the witch. "My soup's almost ready."

They were stuck in the witch's hut until the cauldron was empty.

"I feel sick," groaned Peg on the way back to the coach.

"Well, you shouldn't have had three bowls then," said Fred.

I poured mine into a plant pot.

"I was being polite! I didn't want to hurt the witch's feelings."

"That was very kind of you, Peg," said Prince Patrick, smiling at her.

"Where are we going now?" asked Fred.

"Now I have the witch's test, I can finally find a real princess," said the prince. "We're off to meet Princess Prunella. Check the map, Fred."

Princess Map

N
W   E
S

Princess Prudence

Princess Prunella

Princess Pavlova

Princess Primrose

Chapter 3

Princess Prunella

Princess Prunella was very excited to see the prince.

"You must come and stay in my castle," she cried.

She raced over the bridge, dragging Prince Patrick with her. "Hurry! Hurry!" she called to her servants.

He's perfect. We'll be married in no time.

"I want you to prepare the best bedchambers for the prince and Fred."

"Excuse me," said Peg,
struggling with all the luggage.
"Where am I to sleep?"

"Maids belong in the attic,"
replied the princess, haughtily.
"There might be a few mice
there, but I'm sure you'll cope."

Peg went to her room. It was cold and damp. She could hear mice scuttling about, squeaking.

Meanwhile, Fred and the prince were in the grand dining room with Princess Prunella.

"You're being very kind," said Prince Patrick, "but what about Peg? Is she eating in the kitchen?"

The princess looked shocked. "Your beastly little maid? You can't expect *me* to bother with *her*."

"I'm afraid we must leave," said Prince Patrick. "You're not a real princess after all."

"Oh yes I am!" cried Princess Prunella.

"Oh no you're not!" shouted Fred. "You've failed the first real princess test."

Rats!

"Real princesses are polite to everyone," explained Prince Patrick, "and you've just been rude to Peg."

Chapter 4

Princess Pavlova

"I won't give up!" said Prince Patrick. "There must be a real princess somewhere..."

"According to this map, there's a Princess Pavlova next door. Let's try her," Fred suggested.

Princess Pavlova greeted them all very politely.

"What a pleasure to have you here," she said. "Welcome to my castle."

Thank you, Your Highness.

"She's passed the politeness test," thought the prince. "Now what's the next one..."

"Fred!" he cried, "I have a plan. I'm going to dress up as a beggar and see if Princess Pavlova is kind to me."

"Try out your disguise on Peg first," said Fred, "to make sure it works."

Prince Patrick found Peg sitting on a tree stump, about to eat an apple.

I'm a hungry beggar. Have you any food for me?

"Oh you poor thing!" Peg cried, when she saw him. "Here, have my apple."

31

Prince Patrick was very
pleased with himself. "Excellent!
It works," he shouted, throwing
off his disguise.

It's you!

"What are you doing?"
asked Peg. But the prince
was already knocking on the
castle door, to try the test on
Princess Pavlova.

A servant answered.

"Is someone there?" called Princess Pavlova.

"It's a beggar, Your Highness."

"We've got nothing for him," snapped the princess. "Tell him to go away."

And he smells.

Prince Patrick turned away.

"She's not a real princess," he thought. "A real princess is both polite *and* kind – even to beggars."

A real princess

I'll never be married.

"I give up," said the prince, with a sigh. "I don't think there's a real princess anywhere. We may as well go home."

They got ready for the long journey back to the palace. Everyone was glum, even the horses.

I bet Cook hasn't forgotten about the pudding I burned.

The coach arrived at the palace just in time. A huge storm was brewing.

Peg was sent straight
to the kitchens in disgrace.
"You've got hundreds of
dishes to wash," scolded
the cook. "They've
been piling up since
you left."

Prince Patrick and Fred went
to find the king and queen.
Outside, rain began beating
against the windows. Streaks
of lightning lit up the sky.

Just then, there was a knock
on the door.

"There is a Princess Primrose
to see you, Your Highness,"
said the footman.

Not another one!

A beautiful princess stepped
into the room. She was wet from
the rain and shaking with cold.

"I'm so sorry to trouble
you," she said politely,
"but my coach has
broken down."

37

"No trouble at all," said Prince Patrick quickly. "Why don't you stay the night at our castle? We'll fix your coach in the morning."

Thank you! I must give you something in return.

"She acts like a real princess," thought the prince, "but I must be sure."

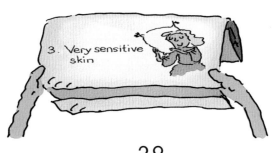

3. Very sensitive skin

He asked the servants to prepare Princess Primrose's bedroom.

"I want twenty mattresses on the bed," ordered Prince Patrick, "and a pea at the very bottom."

Here's your bed, Your Highness.

It's rather high...

Peg didn't get to bed that night. She had to finish washing the dishes.

The next morning, Princess
Primrose came down for
breakfast, looking refreshed.

"How did you sleep?" asked
Prince Patrick.

I slept like
a baby.

"I loved all those mattresses,"
the princess said. "It was the
most comfortable bed."

40

Prince Patrick sighed. "A real princess would have felt that pea," he thought. He waved goodbye to Princess Primrose as soon as breakfast was over.

Another fake one!

She's not good enough for my Patrick.

It was Peg's job to clean the princess's bedroom. Slowly, she climbed up the ladder, yawning with each step.

"I'll just lie down for a moment," Peg thought, "before I start cleaning up."

Zzzzzzzz

In no time at all, she was fast asleep.

An hour later, Peg woke
with a start.

"Ow!" she said. "There's
something really lumpy in this
bed. I'm getting down."

Ooh. It's a long
way.

But as she leaned over, she
knocked the ladder. It clattered
to the ground.

"Drat!" Peg cried. "I'm stuck."

"Help!" she shouted, as loudly as she could, "I'm stuck. Please... HELP!"

Everyone rushed into the bedroom.

"What are you doing up there?" Prince Patrick called.

"I was supposed to be cleaning," said Peg, "but I was so tired I fell asleep."

"And there's something horribly hard in this bed," she added. "I'm covered in bruises."

This can only mean one thing.

"I can't believe it!" cried the prince. "You were polite to the witch, kind to a beggar and now you've felt a pea under twenty mattresses. *You* must be a real princess!"

He raced up the ladder. "Peg, will you marry me?"

Peg gasped. "You want to marry *me*, a palace maid? Yes please!"

A maid?

But a princess at heart!

"Three cheers for Princess Peg," shouted Fred, and everyone cheered.

So Prince Patrick finally married his real princess. He put the pea in a glass case in the palace museum for everyone to see.

It may still be there today...

The Princess and the Pea was first told by Hans Christian Andersen. He was born in Denmark in 1805, the son of a poor shoemaker. He left home at fourteen to seek his fortune and became famous all over the world as a writer of fairy tales.

Cinderella

Retold by Susanna Davidson

Illustrated by
Fabiano Fiorin

Designed by Russell Punter
and Katarina Dragoslavic

Contents

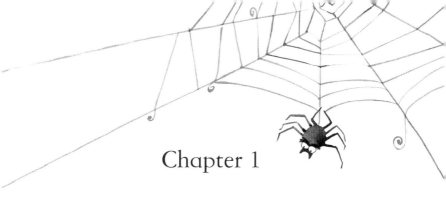

Chapter 1

Invitation to a Ball

"Cinderella!" shouted her
stepmother, looking up from
a letter. "Come and clean my
bedroom at once."

"Yes, Stepmother," Cinderella called from the kitchen, where she was making lunch. Her stepsisters had ordered their usual revolting dishes.

"Well, I've made the sausage trifle," Cinderella thought to herself. "The cabbage and custard pie will just have to wait."

She picked up her
broom and made
her way to the
stairs. But her
stepsisters
were blocking
the way.

"What's little Cinders doing
today then?" teased Griselda.

"She's sweeping away cobwebs,
like a servant," sneered Grimella.

"Get on with it then, servant girl," said Griselda. Just then, Cinderella's stepmother appeared.

"Griselda, Grimella," she cried. "I have the most exciting news. The Prince is giving a Christmas Ball and you're invited."

"We'll dress you in the finest clothes – only the best for my beautiful darlings. Isn't that right, dear?" she said to Cinderella's father.

Cinderella gripped her broom hard. "May I go to the Ball as well?" she asked, in a scared whisper.

"You? Go to the Ball?" said her stepmother. "You must be joking. You belong in the kitchen."

Cinderella turned to her father, but he coughed and looked away. "He's too scared of Stepmother to help me," thought Cinderella. "If only I could go to the Ball..."

Chapter 2

A surprise visit

"We'll be the most beautiful girls there," chorused the stepsisters.

"I'm sure the Prince will want to marry one of you," said their mother, proudly.

"Now, Cinderella," she went on, "as a special treat and since it's nearly Christmas…"

"Yes?" Cinderella cried.

"You may help Griselda and Grimella choose their dresses."

All that week, boot-makers, dressmakers, wig-makers and hairdressers streamed through the door.

Cinderella tried to make
her stepsisters look as pretty
as possible. It wasn't easy.

Grimella wanted to wear a
hat decorated with stuffed birds.
Griselda chose a lime green dress
with yellow spots.

"What about feathers, rather than stuffed birds, Grimella?" Cinderella suggested politely. "And Griselda, I think the yellow dress suited you better."

Shut up, Cinders!

"What would you know?" said Grimella. "But you might be right. We must look grander than everyone else. Sew on lots of rubies and ribbons."

Cinderella worked all day and all night, putting the finishing touches to their outfits.

Hurry up, Cinderella.

At last they were ready. Cinderella's stepsisters gazed at themselves in the mirror.

"Don't we look gorgeous!" they shrieked. "We'll be the finest ladies at the Ball."

"Oh my Tinkerbells, you look wonderful," their mother gasped. "Let's go! The coach is here. Cinderella – put up the Christmas decorations while we're gone."

The front door was opened. There was a swish of skirts and a blast of cold air. Then Cinderella was left alone.

As she struggled with the Christmas tree, tears blurred her eyes. "Oh!" she sobbed, getting tangled in tinsel. "I wish – I *wish* I could go to the Ball."

A loud crash in the chimney made Cinderella look up. There, in the fireplace, covered in soot, was her godmother.

Chapter 3

Fantastic Felicity

"Godmother Felicity," cried Cinderella, "whatever are you doing in our chimney?"

"I missed the door," Felicity replied airily.

"But I haven't seen you since I was ten," said Cinderella.

"I've been with Sleeping Beauty, my other godchild," explained Felicity. "But she wouldn't wake up, so it was rather dull."

"Have you been crying, Cinders?" asked Felicity, looking at her closely.

"Yes! I wanted to go to the Ball, but I'm not allowed."

"Well, you can wipe those tears away, girlie. Fantastic Felicity is here to help. Now, go to the garden and fetch me a large pumpkin."

"Great," thought Cinderella, "my stepsisters are at the Ball and I'm picking up pumpkins for my crazy godmother."

"Here you are," Cinderella said, a few minutes later. "It's the biggest one."

"Jolly good," Felicity replied. "This shouldn't take long."

Now... what was the spell?

"Um, Felicity..." said Cinderella.

"Yes dear?" said Felicity.

"Why are you waving that stick around?"

"This isn't a stick, Cinderella," her godmother replied. "It's a wand. The time has come to tell you a great secret. Your godmother is a fairy!"

Really?

"Watch!" she went on. Felicity flicked her wand at the pumpkin and cried out, "Abracadabra, cadabra cadeen!"

Cinderella waited. Nothing happened. "I don't know much about fairies," Cinderella said, "but shouldn't you be using the other end of your wand?"

Well spotted, Cinderella!

"Silly me!" said Felicity. "Soot on the brain. Let's try again."

There was a wonderful tinkle of music and a shower of sparks. In the place of the pumpkin stood a beautiful golden coach.

Cinderella gasped. "You really can do magic!"

"Yes," said Felicity, "and this is just the beginning. Now, where's your mousetrap?"

"Under the sink," said Cinderella. Felicity peered in.

"Six mice, one fat rat, all alive. Excellent. Open the mousetrap door, Cinderella."

Kazaam!

As each of the mice came out, Felicity gave them a little tap with her wand.

One by one, the mice were transformed into fine white horses. The rat became a rosy-cheeked coachman, with very large whiskers.

"Now I need six lizards," said Felicity. "Hmm... I expect there'll be some behind your watering can."

"There are!" said Cinderella, handing them to her godmother. In a flash, the lizards became footmen.

At your s-s-s-service, Cinderella.

They were dressed in glistening green and looked as if they'd been footmen all their lives.

"There you are, Cinderella," said Felicity, sounding rather pleased with herself. "Now you can go to the Ball."

I'll be off now.

"But I can't go in these rags!" Cinderella cried out.

Felicity touched Cinderella
with her wand. A moment
later, her rags turned into
a dazzling dress of gold
and silver.

On her feet
was a perfect pair
of little glass slippers.

"There's just one problem," said Felicity. "You must leave before twelve. On the last stroke of midnight, my magic will begin to fade."

"I promise," Cinderella replied, climbing into the coach. "And thank you so much!" she called, as the horses swept her away.

Chapter 4

At the Ball

When Cinderella entered
the ballroom, everyone
fell silent. Then slowly,
a whisper went
around the room.

Who can
she be?

"Who's that beautiful girl?" the ladies wondered. "She must be a princess."

A voice next to Cinderella almost made her jump. It was the Prince. "May I have this dance?" he asked.

Cinderella and the Prince twirled across the floor. "She's so graceful," said the other ladies. "And look at her dress! Have you ever seen anything so delicate?"

Ignore her!

"The Prince is only being polite," said Grimella. "He'd much rather dance with me."

Cinderella was enjoying herself so much, she forgot to watch the time. As the Prince whirled her around the room, she caught sight of the clock.

The time!

"Oh no!" she said. "It's almost midnight. I must go."

Cinderella pulled away from the Prince and ran across the dance floor. The Prince raced after her. "Come back," he called.

I don't even know your name.

But Cinderella had disappeared into the darkness.

"Have you seen a girl in a gold and silver dress?" the Prince asked the palace guard.

"No," said the guard. "A girl ran past a moment ago, but she was dressed in rags."

I've lost her.

The Prince turned back to the palace with a sigh. Then something on the steps caught his eye. "Her glass slipper!" he cried.

The glass slipper

Cinderella ran
home as fast as
she could. She arrived
just before her stepsisters.

"How was the Ball?"
Cinderella asked.

"It was very grand," said
Griselda. "Far too grand for
the likes of you."

I'm sure the
Prince is in love
with me.

Cinderella smiled, but she
said nothing.

The next morning, the entire
street was woken by the shout
of a town crier, who was
followed by a messenger.

By the order of his
royal highness, the
Prince, every girl in the
kingdom must try on this
glass slipper. The
Prince will marry its
true owner.

Cinderella's stepmother flung open the front door and grabbed the messenger.

"One of my girls will fit this shoe," she said proudly, "and then I'll be queen."

Griselda couldn't even fit her big toe in the shoe. She pushed until her foot was bright red.

"Give it to me!" shouted Grimella, and snatched the glass slipper from her sister. Grimella rammed half her foot in the shoe, but then it got stuck.

"Squeeze, Grimella," shrieked her mother. "You're not trying hard enough."

"I'm trying as hard as I can, Mama," said Grimella, with a grunt.

Ow!

"You useless child," cried her mother. She wrenched the slipper off Grimella's foot and flung it at the messenger. "Off you go then," she snapped.

The messenger cleared his throat. "Excuse me, ma'am," he said, "but my strict orders are that every young lady is to try on the shoe." He looked directly at Cinderella.

What about this girl?

"What?" said Grimella. "She's just a servant. You needn't bother with her."

Cinderella's father coughed. "Actually..." he began.

"Shut up you stupid man," interrupted the stepmother.

"...Cinderella has as much right to try on the slipper as anyone," he went on, bravely.

"Oh Papa!" said Cinderella. She walked over to the messenger and slipped on the shoe. It was a perfect fit.

"No!" shrieked Griselda and Grimella.

"She can't be a princess," shouted their mother. "I won't allow it."

This is all your fault.

"Get out!" she screamed at the messenger. "I want you to pretend this never happened."

With one swift movement,
the messenger swept off his hat
and cloak. Everyone in the
room gasped. It was the Prince.

He strode over to Cinderella.
"I would have searched my
kingdom for you," he said.
"Will you marry me?"

Cinderella smiled. "Oh yes!" she replied.

At that moment, there was a puff of smoke and Felicity flew into the room.

She held her wand above her head and a starry mist swirled around them all. "Time for a little more magic," she declared.

Felicity flicked her wand and gave Cinderella a dress even more beautiful than the one she had worn to the Ball.

"My princess!" said the Prince, and swept Cinderella off to his palace. Cinderella and the Prince were married the very next day...

...and lived happily ever after.
Griselda and Grimella
were not so happy.

We wanted
to marry the
Prince.

Their mother never stopped
scolding them. "It's all your
fault for having such big feet,"
she told them.

There are over 700 versions of Cinderella.
Cinderella has also been known as Rashin Coatie
in Scotland, Aschenputtel in Germany, Zezolla in
Italy, and Yeh-hsien in China. This version is from
a retelling by Charles Perrault, a French writer
who lived in the seventeenth century.

The
Twelve Dancing Princesses

Retold by Emma Helbrough

Illustrated by
Anna Luraschi

Designed by Russell Punter
and Natacha Goransky

Contents

Chapter 1

Family trouble

There were once twelve
beautiful princesses, all with
long, flowing hair and short,
fiery tempers.

Their father, the king, was a grumpy old man who didn't believe in having fun.

In fact, he believed that princesses should be seen and not heard.

Ballroom →

NO
ENTRY

The princesses strongly disagreed.

101

The thing they argued
about most was dancing.
Their father hated it, but
the princesses loved it...

so whenever
he wasn't
looking,
they danced
anyway.

Chapter 2

The sisters' secret

The girls slept in a tall tower
with their beds side by side.

Every night, the king locked
the tower door, so that they
couldn't sneak out.

Sleep well,
my dears.

One morning, when the door was unlocked, the princesses were still asleep.

As the maid went to wake them, she noticed their shoes were lying in a soggy pile on the floor.

How strange!

The shoes were worn out.

When the king heard about the shoes, he was furious. "Those girls have been out dancing," he spluttered.

Bring my daughters here... NOW!

Yes, sire.

"Princesses should not be out dancing all night!" he yelled at them. "You need your beauty sleep. You should all be ashamed of yourselves."

The girls weren't ashamed in the least. What's more, they wouldn't tell him how they had escaped or where they had been.

The next morning, it was clear that the princesses had been out again. The same thing happened seven nights in a row.

The king didn't know what to do.

Then he had a brilliant idea.

He decided that the first man to discover where his daughters went each night could marry one of them. Posters went up across the land.

Fed up with your job? Feel like a challenge?

Solve a royal mystery and win big prizes!!

Win your own kingdom and marry a genuine princess!

Interested? Drop in to the castle for further details.

No time wasters please.

Chapter 3

Taking the challenge

The first man to take up the king's challenge was brave Prince Marcus.

"By the way, there is one small catch," the king told him. "If you fail, I'll cut off your head!"

Um...okay... no problem, your majesty.

That night, Prince Marcus
was taken to the tower and put
in a room next to the princesses.

Very
comfortable
indeed!

They made him
very welcome.
One even
brought him
a cup of hot,
milky cocoa.

As Prince Marcus drank the cocoa, he began to feel sleepy.

He tried splashing cold water on his face, but that didn't work.

Soon he was fast asleep and snoring loudly.

Next morning, the princesses' shoes were worn out again. Prince Marcus had failed – and the king wasn't joking about chopping off his head.

Take him away!

Many more princes and
noble knights came forward.
But they were all fooled by the
princesses' sweet smiles...

and their offer
of hot cocoa.

Chapter 4

Ralph and Rascal

One day, a magician named
Ralph and his pet dog, Rascal,
were passing the castle.

Ralph noticed one of the king's posters and decided to find out more.

This could be interesting, Rascal!

When he saw Ralph, the king looked doubtful. But he was desperate to know what the girls were up to, so he agreed to let Ralph try.

I'll chop off your head if you fail, you know.

Yes, but I won't fail...

Night came and Ralph was put in the same room where the others had stayed.

"Hello! I'm Amy," said the youngest. "He's nice," she whispered to her sisters. "I don't want him to die because of us. Maybe we shouldn't go out tonight..."

Her sisters ignored her.

119

A few minutes later, Annabel, the eldest sister, brought Ralph a cup of cocoa. But Ralph was a wise magician. He knew what she was up to.

He pretended to drink the
cocoa. Then, when Annabel
wasn't looking, he poured it
into Rascal's bowl.
Rascal was
delighted.

Ralph yawned. "I think I'll
just put my feet up for a few
minutes," he told Annabel.

Then, with an even bigger
yawn, he pretended to fall
fast asleep.

Annabel crept back to her sisters. "He's asleep," she whispered. "Let's get ready!"

They put on their sparkliest ball dresses...

and new shoes. The princesses shimmered like a rainbow.

123

With the last button buttoned and the last bow tied, the girls stood by their beds. Annabel pulled back a dusty, old rug in the corner of the room to reveal a secret trap door. The hinges creaked as she pulled it open.

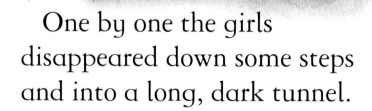

One by one the girls disappeared down some steps and into a long, dark tunnel.

Ralph on the trail

When the princesses were out
of sight, Ralph quickly
entered their room.

He clicked his
fingers and a
cloak appeared.
With a second
click, Ralph
vanished.

Carefully, he
tiptoed down the
steps into the tunnel.

It didn't take long for him to
catch up with the princesses.

Ralph tried to walk quietly,
but it wasn't easy. At one
point he stepped on Amy's
dress. She jumped and turned
around, but there was no
one there...

A few moments later Ralph stepped on a twig. Now Amy was convinced that someone was following them. Her sisters didn't believe her.

At the end of the tunnel they came to an astonishing row of trees.

Some of the trees glistened with silver...

some with gold...

and some with sparkling diamonds.

Ralph had never seen trees like them. While the princesses carried on, he gently broke off a twig from each tree.

Up ahead, the princesses had stopped before a lake. It stood in the shadow of a beautiful castle.

Twelve boats were
waiting at the edge
of the lake and in
each boat sat a
handsome prince.

Each prince rowed a princess
across the lake.

131

Ralph sneaked into the boat carrying Amy. When they reached the other side, a band began to play.

The princesses danced until
their feet were sore and
the soles of their shoes
were worn through.

As the sun rose, they limped home. "Our nights of dancing are still safe – unlike poor Ralph's head!" said Annabel, yawning. Amy looked upset.

Chapter 6

A shock for the king

The king was having breakfast when Ralph strolled in. "Good morning, your majesty," said Ralph brightly.

"I suppose you've come to tell me you failed too," sighed the king.

"Ah, but I didn't, sire," Ralph replied. Waving the twigs, he told the king what he'd seen.

The mystery is solved!

136

"This all sounds very unlikely," grumbled the king, when Ralph had finished. "Are you sure you're not just making it up to save your head?"

He decided to call for
Annabel. When she saw the
three twigs in his hand, she
looked horrified.

One look at her face told the
king all he needed to know.
"Dancing is banned!" he declared.

The princesses sobbed and wailed when they heard their secret had been discovered.

"What will we do?" they cried. "Life is so dull without dancing."

This is the worst day of my life.

But there was nothing they could do.

True to his word, the king let Ralph marry one of his daughters. "I'd like Amy," Ralph said, "if she'll have me. She's the sweetest of all."

I'm sure you'll both be very happy.

Amy and Ralph's wedding was a joyful occasion. Even the king couldn't stop smiling. "I have a surprise for you," he whispered to Amy.

The king led her to the
ballroom and Amy gasped.
Hundreds of candles lit up
the dance floor and in
the corner a band was
playing a lively tune.

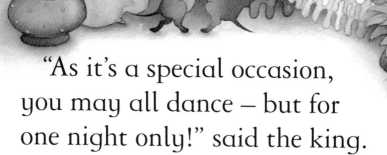

"As it's a special occasion,
you may all dance – but for
one night only!" said the king.

142

"Oh, how wonderful!" cried Amy and her sisters, grabbing partners. They were all still dancing the following night.

"I thought I said one night only!" said the king, but he smiled. Ralph had worked some more of his magic.

The Twelve Dancing Princesses was first written down by two brothers, Jacob and Wilhelm Grimm. They lived in Germany in the early 1800s and together they retold hundreds of fairy tales.

First published in 2006 by Usborne Publishing Ltd., Usborne House, 83-85 Saffron Hill, London EC1N 8RT, England. www.usborne.com
Copyright © 2006, 2004 Usborne Publishing Ltd.

144